Kill the Bully

A Story about Gun Control

Based on a True Story

Anthony J Placito

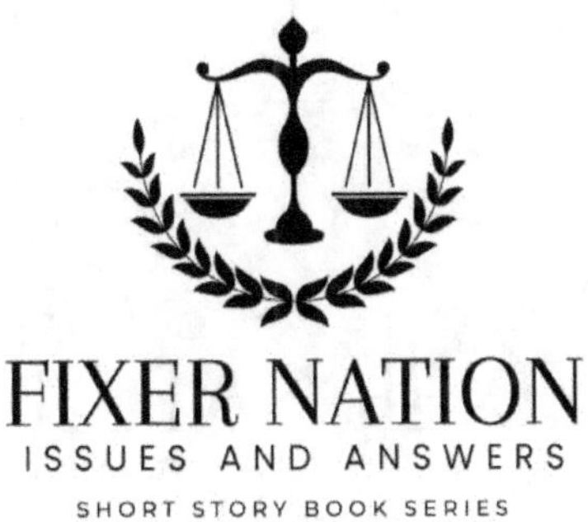

FIXER NATION

ISSUES AND ANSWERS

SHORT STORY BOOK SERIES

Our Mission

Fixer Nation (FN) is your modern-day source for clear, reliable solutions to everyday questions and challenges. Whether you're facing a dilemma or seeking clarity on an issue, Fixer Nation provides unbiased insights, practical tools, and valuable resources to help you find the right answers—and discover who or what can truly be the Fixer in your situation.

Our Vision

Fixer Nation (FN) will be the leading global platform for positivity, health, and wellness—uniquely designed to help every member navigate life's challenges, achieve their goals, and feel genuinely supported. Not everyone is welcome—only those ready to rise.

We envision a world where personal transformation is powered by collective strength, and every individual feels empowered to break through their barriers.

Our Values

At Fixer Nation, we believe in empowering individuals through guidance and support. We lead with positivity, prioritize purpose over popularity, and foster a safe, judgment-free space. Every journey is personal, so we tailor content to your unique goals—while cultivating a high-standard community focused on authentic growth.

Congratulations on Investing in Yourself!
Welcome to Fixer Nation — The Health Club for Your
Mind, Body & Soul

You've taken a powerful step forward by joining the Fixer Nation community and purchasing your book — your personal guide to turning life's issues into answers.

Now it's time to activate your FREE 90-day membership inside Fixer Nation: The Positivity, Health, and Wellness Network. The health club for your mind, body and soul.

A Health Club Like No Other
This isn't just another program — it's a movement.

Fixer Nation is where positivity meets purpose, where personal growth meets daily action, and where your best self takes center stage.

Your journey begins with our exclusive Morning Boost — 7 Daily
Success Rituals that help you:

- Strengthen your mindset and emotional resilience
- Fuel your body with purpose and positivity
- Build lasting gratitude, focus, and confidence
- Create habits that lead to success and joy
- Connect with a community that lifts you higher every day

Your Morning Boost Experience

Each day, you'll receive inspiration, humor, reflection, and action

— everything you need to align your mind, body, and soul with
your highest potential.

This is where small steps become big breakthroughs — where you
learn to live intentionally and joyfully.

* Your 90-Day Free Membership Includes

* Daily Morning Boost (7 Success Rituals)
* Exclusive Fixer Nation Content Library
* Health & Wellness Tools for Body and Mind
* Access to the Fixer Nation Positivity Community

What Members Say

"This changed my mornings — and my mindset."
"Fixer Nation reminds me daily that I have what it takes."

You Were Born a Fixer — You Just Don't Know It Yet

Your book opened the door — now this 90-day experience will
show you what's possible when positivity becomes your lifestyle.

Start Your Journey Today

You've already made the investment in yourself.

Now claim what you've earned — your 90 days of growth, clarity, and empowerment.

[Scan the QR Code and enter coupon code 90dayfreetrial to Start Your Free 90 Days]

Your transformation begins now — only at **Fixer Nation: The Positivity, Health & Wellness Network- Welcome to The Health Club for Your Mind, Body and Soul**

Acknowledgments

This project has been a significant undertaking, and I am deeply grateful for the support and encouragement of the many individuals who made it possible. I would like to extend my sincere thanks to all of you.

It has been an honor and a privilege to work with the Fixer Nation Business Development Services Team. I sincerely thank them for their guidance, constant supervision, and invaluable insights throughout this process. Their willingness to share their vast knowledge helped me gain a deeper understanding of the project and its complexities, ultimately enabling me to excel and succeed.

I would also like to express my heartfelt gratitude to my parents, family members, and friends for their unwavering support, encouragement, and guidance throughout my journey. Their belief in me has been instrumental in the successful completion of this stage of my ongoing journey.

Finally, my appreciation extends to my colleagues and everyone who has generously shared their time, expertise, and efforts in bringing this project to fruition. Your contributions have been invaluable, and I am truly grateful.

Dedication

This book is dedicated to you, the reader.

If you have a problem, you've come to the right place to solve it.

FIXER NATION *CREDO:

We believe there are no problems in life—only issues and answers.

You are *"The Fixer"*—and together, *We are "Fixer Nation"*.

Fixer Nation was created for you and it's more than a social media platform—it's a community designed to help people become the best versions of themselves.

Our network connects like-minded, goal-oriented individuals who are committed to improving their lives with the people, companies, and tools that can assist them on their journey toward achieving their goals.

Fixer Nation is your community where real people engage in real discussions about positivity, health, and personal growth. This is a space for those who want to excel, not just exist.

It is the premier community for those committed to thriving in life.

We are Fixer Nation!

Credo - A set of beliefs that influences the way you live.

About the Author

With 25 years of experience in the education market, Anthony J. Placito has dedicated his career to providing technology-driven solutions for schools, developing curricula for students from kindergarten through university.

Throughout his journey, Anthony recognized a deeper need—to offer guidance and insight into the everyday challenges people face. He believes that in life, there are no problems, only issues and answers. We are a nation of Fixers not victims.

Inspired by this philosophy, he created Fixer Nation – Issues & Answers, a short story series designed to engage young and mature minds alike, offering thought-provoking perspectives on life's challenges and potential solutions.

Expanding on this mission, Anthony also founded Fixer Nation – The Positivity, Health & Wellness Network, an exclusive members-only social platform dedicated to personal growth, support, and empowerment. This safe place was built to help individuals become the best version of themselves—every single day.

Welcome to Fixer Nation.

Your safe place to grow.

It was built just for you.

Cheers.

Chapter 1 - "The Fixer is Born"

It was a cold, wintry night in the middle of a severe snowstorm in Syracuse, NY. It had been snowing for two days straight, and the towering snowbanks at street corners made it nearly impossible to see oncoming traffic at stop signs and traffic lights. The snowplows simply couldn't keep up with the historic storm.

Sarah was nine months pregnant and could go into labor at any moment. Her husband, David, was on high alert, deeply concerned about how they would get to the hospital given the worsening conditions.

They couldn't afford an ambulance, and their car was far from reliable.

David had just arrived home from work, tense from the hazardous drive. He stepped through the front door, brushing the snow off his coat before removing his hat and gloves. After kissing his wife on the cheek and hugging his two-year-old daughter, Lily, he asked Sarah, "How was your day?"

She smiled. "Little Lily had fun playing with her toys and was pretty quiet today. But this little one inside me doesn't seem to want to stay put for long."

David chuckled. "Well, that's okay—just as long as the baby doesn't come tonight."

Sarah smirked. "Why?"

"I think we'd have some trouble getting to the hospital if we had to go tonight," David admitted.

"We could make it if we take it slow," he added, though there was hesitation in his voice. "But at this rate, the snow could easily double or triple our travel time."

Sarah's expression turned serious. "Well... I've been feeling strong kicks all day, and I think this little guy wants out tonight. Maybe we should just go now and camp out in the hospital waiting room," she joked.

The moment the words left her mouth, she let out a sharp scream, bent over in pain, and gasped, "Well, we have to go now!"

Without hesitation, David sprang into action. "Okay, sit down right here. I'll grab Lily. Where's your hospital bag?"

"In our bedroom—inside the closet door, on the right."

David dashed to the bedroom, grabbed the bag, and rushed back to the kitchen to bundle Lily into her winter clothes. Within minutes, they were on their way to the hospital, but the journey was slow and treacherous on the snow-covered roads.

Abandoned cars sat in ditches, while others had been in accidents. Police lights flashed, snowplow lights blinked, and through it all, Lily —wide-eyed and curious—asked, "Mama, Papa, are any of those lights Santa's sleigh?"

She was still new to the magic of Christmas and hadn't quite grasped that it only came once a year. As far as she was concerned, a snowstorm plus flashing lights could only mean one thing—Santa Claus was on his way.

In a way, Lily was right—something exciting was happening. But Santa had already come and gone two months earlier. It was now February.

For over 40 minutes, David drove cautiously, never exceeding 15–25 mph. Finally, they reached the bottom of St. Joseph's Hospital Hill. Sarah's contractions were coming faster and stronger now.

"This is the hill I warned you about," David muttered. It was the only road leading to the emergency room entrance.

He turned onto the incline and immediately started talking to the car, as he often did when it needed encouragement. He called it King—or "Kingy" when it required extra coaxing.

"Come on, King, you can do this," he urged as the car crawled up the hill. "Don't spin your tires—grip, grip, grip!"

Then, halfway up, the traffic light turned red.

David groaned, shaking his head in frustration. "No, no, no… no, no, no… no, no, no!" His words took on the rhythm of a Christmas carol.

From the backseat, Lily piped up, "Dad, are you singing Christmas songs?"

David forced a chuckle. "No, honey, Daddy just really needs to get up this hill."

Sarah shot him a warning look—a silent plea not to scare Lily. Just drive.

The light turned green. David pressed the gas. The tires spun in place, failing to grip the icy pavement. Then, slowly, the car began sliding backward—first a little, then more. He slammed the brakes, but it only made things worse. The car skidded sideways, veering toward the edge of the road.

Panic surged through him.

He jammed the car into park, took a deep breath, and turned to his wife and daughter. "Sit still. I'll be right back."

David got out of the car to assess the situation. As he walked around it, he noticed a sled in the front yard of a nearby house, just a few feet from where their car had come to a stop on the side of the road.

Realizing that their car had no chance of making it up the hill, David grabbed the sled, ran to the passenger side, and yelled to Sarah, "We're not going to make it up the hill with the car! Get in the sled with Lily—I'll have to pull you up."

Sarah, still in the throes of labor, looked at him anxiously. "No, David, we're never gonna make it. You can't pull us up that hill."

"Yeah, well, you better hope I can," David shot back, "or we'll be having this baby in the middle of a snowstorm on the side of the road."

Without further argument, David sprang into action. He helped Sarah out of the car, got her as comfortable as possible in the sled, and covered her with a blanket. "Lily, come on, honey. Sit in the front of the sled and get under the blanket with Mommy."

Lily obeyed without question, snuggling close to her mother.

David grabbed the rope attached to the sled and started climbing. The snowstorm had intensified, the wind whipping against him. He moved slowly, struggling against the icy incline. His boots slipped repeatedly, and when he tried to transition into a slow jog, he lost his footing and fell.

Lily giggled, thinking her father was just playing in the snow.

Despite the grueling effort, David pressed on, pulling his wife and daughter toward safety. By the time they reached the hospital entrance, all three of them were breathless, their cheeks flushed a rosy red, their noses running from the cold.

As soon as David pulled the sled through the emergency room doors, he shouted, "We're having a baby over here!"

The hospital staff sprang into action, rushing Sarah into admissions and then straight to the delivery room.

Inside, the scene was familiar yet extraordinary—doctors and nurses moving swiftly, a midwife coaching, a husband murmuring words of encouragement to his wife.

And then, a moment of stillness.

From the instant we enter this world, there is always something that needs fixing.

The doctor gave the newborn a firm pat on the bottom. The baby let out a loud, sharp cry—its first breath.

And as the people in the room celebrated the birth of new life, the journey of fixing things had already begun.

From our very first breath, to our first meal, to our first diaper change—there is always something that needs to be fixed. Yet, in those moments, we have no answers and no understanding of what needs to be done.

We just know one thing: we need it to be fixed.

And so, we seek the one who can fix it.

Who is The Fixer?

As we grow, we continue to discover more things that need fixing. Throughout childhood and our formative years, we learn who our fixers are and how to rely on them. As newborns, we cry for attention, knowing instinctively that someone will respond to our needs. As we transition into adulthood, we develop our own ways of seeking out The Fixer.

But one day, inevitably, we encounter a problem—an issue—that cannot be solved by the fixers we have always turned to. The people and solutions that once worked so effortlessly no longer do.

Life presents us with new problems—some that we can easily fix, drawing from the lessons we've learned along the way. But others seem impossible, obstacles so overwhelming that we begin to doubt if they can ever be overcome.

We are faced with life's issues, and often, we have no answers.

Suddenly, we find ourselves in a world of daily challenges, both big and small. We manage to fix most of them, thanks to what life has already taught us. But sooner or later, we reach a moment of realization—deep in our minds and even deeper in our hearts— where we know one undeniable truth:

We need The Fixer.

We turn to our higher power. We confide in our parents. We seek therapy. We talk to our priests, our friends, our loved ones. Or worse, we do nothing at all. In each case, the goal is the same—to find a fix. Or, failing that, to convince ourselves that no fix exists. And maybe we're right.

Life is a constant cycle of issues and answers, a never-ending search for solutions. From the moment we take our first breath, we begin solving problems at every stage of life. Along the way, we rely on the fixers who are available to us—Mom, Dad, our primary caretaker, siblings, grandparents, relatives, religion, self-help books, therapy, seminars.

Society often associates the term The Fixer with something else entirely. A mafia enforcer. A hired gun who eliminates problems—for a price. Or the guy who's called in after the damage is done, cleaning up messes and making sure no one ever finds out.

Some people spend their entire lives searching for The Fixer, believing that someone, somewhere, holds the key to solving their problems. Some take action. Others do nothing at all. But in the end, what they truly desire is the same—someone or something to fix what feels broken.

The question then becomes:

Who can help me fix this?

Who has the knowledge to solve this problem?

Will this ever be fixed?

Or... is this something that can't be fixed?

What is the one thing I believe in? Or... what should I believe in?

At some point in life, we all ask the same universal question:

Who can fix this? Because I can't.

These days, you can go to YouTube and find a video tutorial on how to fix just about anything. But when it comes to fixing yourself—where do you go? What resource exists for that?

Chapter 2

I made it through the first few years of my life without much trouble—until I started school. Up until then, I had access to Mom and Dad for just about everything, and I spent weekends with my grandparents. Life was simple.

Then came my first week of school, and with it, my first real challenge. It all started at the bus stop—the first time I met my bully. Of course, I didn't know enough back then to recognize that I was being bullied. All I knew was that something about this kid felt... different. He was just *mean.*

His name was Brandon Pierce. I already knew who he was because he lived in our neighborhood, and I'd seen him at church with his mom. My grandma and his mom would exchange polite hellos whenever we passed them going in or out of church.

Brandon was a big kid, bigger than most, and he always had this scowl on his face, like he was mad at the world. I never thought much of it—until the first day of school, when we ended up waiting at the same bus stop.

Trying to be friendly, I asked, "Are you mad about something?"

His reaction was instant and aggressive. His face twisted in anger, and he snapped, "Mind your own business."

That was the first red flag.

When we got on the bus, Brandon sat directly behind me and immediately started tapping my shoulder. Every time I turned around, he'd just point at the kid sitting next to him, acting like he had nothing to do with it. He kept it up the entire ride.

At first, I tried to ignore it, but it got under my skin. And as the days passed, it became clear that Brandon had found something that gave him power—or at least some kind of satisfaction.

The relief I felt when I got off the bus that morning was overwhelming.

But my luck ran out fast.

When we got to school and were assigned to our classrooms, I was stunned to see Brandon Pierce in mine. And then, just when I thought it couldn't get worse, our teacher, Ms. Reynolds, assigned lockers—and Brandon's ended up right next to mine.

No matter where I turned, he was there.

At first, I told myself it was just bad luck. But then lunchtime came, and I knew I was in trouble.

Our teacher had a system—everything was done in alphabetical order. I think it was meant to help us learn the alphabet, but for me, it became a nightmare.

We lined up alphabetically for recess.

For lunch.

For bus routes.

My name is Alex Parker. His is Brandon Pierce.

That meant, every single day, for every single event, I was stuck right next to him.

By the end of that first day, I was horrified. It was obvious that Brandon didn't like me. What I *didn't* know was why.

It was almost as if something else was bothering him—something bigger than me.

Chapter 3

As the days passed, then the weeks, and eventually the months, nothing changed. The daily name-calling started at the bus stop each morning, continued throughout the school day, and even followed me onto the ride home.

I did get occasional breaks—brief moments of relief—when Brandon found someone else to mess with. I felt bad for those kids because I knew exactly how it felt. But at the same time, I couldn't help but be grateful that, at least for a few minutes, he wasn't focused on me.

Our first real confrontation happened in gym class during a dodgeball game. Brandon was one of the biggest guys in our class—actually, *the* biggest—and I was the smallest. Right away, I knew I wanted to be on his team. The last thing I needed was him whipping dodgeballs at me.

But as luck would have it, we ended up on opposite teams.

Now, don't get me wrong—I was small, but I was quick, and I had good reflexes. I could dodge and catch balls pretty well. The game started, and Brandon dominated right away. He went after the boys first, then the girls, and he didn't just hit you—he *punished* you. He threw the ball so hard that it left bright red marks wherever it struck. Some of his shots hit with such force that they knocked kids right off their feet.

While Brandon was busy wreaking havoc, I managed to stay in the game by focusing on his teammates instead.

Then, as fate would have it, it came down to just the two of us.

Brandon hurled the ball at me—fast and hard. I barely managed to block it, and as he ran toward another ball to reload, I threw mine at him as quickly as I could. He tried to leap over it, but my shot caught his leg—his landing leg. He was midair.

He came crashing down onto his butt.

I *got* him.

We won.

The rush I felt in that moment was incredible. My teammates cheered. Brandon's teammates *jeered*.

"He's half your size, and he took you out!" one of them laughed.

It felt so *right* to see Brandon embarrassed for once. He was finally getting a taste of what he put me through every single day—on the bus, in the lunchroom, at our lockers, in gym class. *Now* he would understand how he made people feel.

Surely, he would change after this.

I could not have been more wrong.

If anything, it made things worse.

From that moment on, Brandon became *laser-focused* on making my life miserable. He harassed me at every opportunity— any time he was near me. It didn't matter where we were. He made fun of me in the hallways, in class, even in front of teachers—and sometimes, they *laughed along with him.*

I tried not to let it get to me. I pushed my feelings deep down and convinced myself that if I just ignored it, things would eventually get better.

Then came the day it became *too much.*

That morning, it had rained. By the time I got to the bus stop, puddles covered the pavement. Brandon was already there when I arrived.

Without hesitation, he stomped his foot sideways into a puddle, sending a wave of cold, dirty water all over me.

I was soaking wet.

I climbed onto the bus, found my seat, and stared out the window, blinking back tears. I had to spend the *entire day* in wet clothes, with dripping hair, feeling humiliated.

When we got to school, I went to my locker—right next to *her* locker.

Emily Dawson.

She was a dream girl. Beautiful, smart, kind. And there I was, standing there, completely drenched, looking like a mess.

As if the situation couldn't get worse, kids pointed and laughed at me from the moment I got off the bus. The teasing followed me all the way to my locker and into homeroom.

But Emily… she was different.

She smiled at me. "Good morning, Alex. Did you get caught in the rain on the way to school?"

I forced a small smile. "No… worse. But I'm dealing with it."

She just nodded, still smiling. "Have a nice day." Then she shut her locker and walked away.

I let out a deep sigh and headed to the bathroom to try and dry off.

But just when I thought I'd escaped, there he was.

Brandon.

He was at the sink washing his hands. The second he saw me, he cupped his hands, filled them with water, and flung it right at me.

The laughter erupted instantly.

Once again, I was the punchline to Brandon Pierce's joke.

Chapter 4

It was becoming clear to me that Brandon was different—something was bothering him. But I had no clue what it was or why it involved me.

He was always alone. No one really wanted to be his friend, not because he was quiet, but because he only spoke when he didn't like you. And if you were the unlucky one next to him, that usually meant trouble.

It also seemed like he only acted like a bully when other people were around, like he was putting on a show for someone—or something.

One morning, we arrived at the bus stop at the same time.

My stomach dropped.

I didn't want to be alone with him—it gave him the perfect opportunity to torment me without interruption. I had to do something.

So, I tried to beat him to the punch.

I got myself all worked up, pretending to be furious with my mom. I threw a wild tantrum about having to have a packed lunch for school instead of getting lunch money. I ranted, I stomped, I complained loudly about how much I *hated* my mom's lunches.

That's when something strange happened.

Brandon's expression shifted. His usual smirk faded, and for the first time, he looked at me—not with anger, but with something else. *Pity?*

But it wasn't pity *for me*. That's what was weird.

Then, out of nowhere, he muttered, "Well, at least you have a mother that cares. At least you have a father who isn't constantly drunk and doesn't take out his frustrations on you."

I froze.

I didn't know what to say. I was completely caught off guard. So, like an idiot, I blurted out, "Well… it can't be that bad."

I regretted it instantly.

Brandon's face darkened. Just like that, whatever moment of weakness he had shown was gone, replaced by pure hostility.

From then on, he was relentless. The dodgeball incident had already put me on his radar, but now, with our awkward exchange at the bus stop, I had somehow made things even worse.

Every day turned into the same routine. Different day, same misery.

That day, when we got to school, it didn't take long for him to find me again. As I was opening my locker, Emily was at hers, just a few feet away.

Brandon walked up, shoved me hard against my locker, and snatched my lunch bag from my hands.

"Well, thanks for the lunch," he sneered. "I'll take this today. And your lunch—or your lunch money—tomorrow. And the next day, too."

Emily overheard him and immediately stepped in.

"Come on, Brandon, leave him alone," she said. "Don't you think you hassle him enough?"

Brandon turned to her, his expression shifting into something even nastier. "I could turn my focus on you instead," he said coldly. "You're lucky you're a girl, or I'd make you hand over your lunch money too."

I felt a surge of anger. Without thinking, I stepped between them and placed a hand on Brandon's shoulder.

"Come on, Brandon," I said, trying to keep my voice steady. "Leave her alone. You don't have to be this way. You don't have to be mean all the time—don't you ever laugh or smile?"

I barely saw it coming.

Brandon grabbed my arm, twisted it sharply, and drove me down to my knees. Then, bending down next to me, he whispered into my ear, his grip still tight.

"Don't forget my lunch tomorrow, *Parker*."

The humiliation was unbearable.

My arm throbbed. But worse than that was the burning shame in my chest.

He had humiliated me. *Again.* Right in front of Emily.

And now, I had something else to worry about— Brandon taking my lunch or my lunch money every single day.

It wasn't just about bullying anymore. It wasn't just about getting pushed around or called names. Now, it was physical.

And Emily had seen it all.

I *liked* her. And now, after watching Brandon twist my arm like I was nothing, I knew she probably saw me as weak, too.

At that moment, I only had one thought running through my head.

I had to stop this.

I had to get back at him for everything—for the bullying, for threatening Emily, for *everything* he had done to me.

And then another thought crept in.

I wish I could just kill him.

I wanted him *gone*.

Not just Brandon —but all of them. The teachers who saw what he did and laughed. The students who stood by and did nothing. The ones who even *defended* him when I got caught retaliating.

It seemed like he never got in trouble. And even when he did, it was like he had some secret pass—some permission—to get away with it.

It wasn't fair.

And I was done being his victim.

Chapter 5

I was so upset that I went to my grandpa and asked him to teach me how to use his gun. I wanted to borrow it.

At first, he chuckled and smiled, but then he started asking me questions.

"What would you borrow it for?" he asked.

I explained, "Grandpa, there's this really mean kid at school. His name is Brandon Pierce. He rides my bus and is in all of my classes. Every day, he takes my lunch money or my bagged lunch. If I try to stop him or fight back, he beats me up. He pushes me down, mocks me, and makes everyone laugh at me. And now, he's doing it to a girl named Emily that I really like—a *lot*."

Grandpa paused, then cleared his throat. "Oh… so the final straw was that he embarrassed you in front of little Miss Emily and threatened her?"

I nodded. "Yeah… that's part of it. I just want him *gone*. He harasses me and puts his hands on me *every day*."

Grandpa let out a short laugh and said, "Alright, Alex We'll go to the gun range. I'll teach you how to shoot—and how to kill the bully. If you do well and learn, maybe I'll even buy you your own gun. Don't worry—you won't be the victim anymore."

There was something about his tone. It was almost funny, and it caught my attention.

I thought to myself, *This is great. I am the victim, but I won't be anymore.*

Grandpa continued, "Alright, but you have to promise to listen and do everything I show you. Okay?"

I responded excitedly, "Okay, Grandpa!"

He nodded. "Good. Now, there's a lot more to it than just shooting. You have to learn how to handle the gun properly, how to load it, how to clean it, and how to fire it."

I was hanging onto every word, barely able to contain my excitement.

Then Grandpa added, "But there's one more important thing you have to promise me you'll learn."

"What is it?" I asked eagerly. "If you show me, I *can* do it, and I *will* do it."

He smiled. "Alright. We'll go Saturday morning."

It was Friday, and Grandpa P was picking up my sister and me from school. We spent weekends with my dad's parents, Grandma and Grandpa P. In some ways, I was like Brandon —I came from a broken home. My mom and dad had divorced when I was really young. I lived with my mom during the week, staying with her mother, Grandma W. Then, on weekends, I stayed with my dad's mother, Grandma P.

My dad's last name was Parker, and my mom's last name was Wisniewski. All the grandkids called our grandparents by the first letter of their last names—so they became Grandma and Grandpa P and Grandma W. There was no Grandpa W—he had died before I was born.

When school let out, I rushed outside to meet Grandma P and Grandpa P in the pickup line. Cars and buses lined up next to each other as students poured out of the building.

Most weekends, I wasn't excited about going to my grandparents' house. They lived on the other side of town, far from my school and friends, so I never had anyone to play with.

But *this* weekend was different.

This weekend, I was getting a gun.

At least, that's what I thought.

I jumped into the car, kissed Grandma P on the cheek, and hugged Grandpa P over the seat. "Are we still going to the gun range tomorrow morning?" I asked.

Grandpa grinned. "Yes, we are. But we need to get ready tonight—especially if you're going to use what you learn against your bully. What was his name again?"

"Brandon. Brandon Pierce," I said bitterly. "And he took my lunch again today. And Emily*'s* lunch money, too."

"Ohhh," Grandpa said with a smirk. "Your girlfriend?"

"No! Well… yes. I *want* her to be," I admitted, "but she doesn't know it yet."

Grandma P smiled. "Alright, let's focus on one thing at a time."

Since it was Friday, we had our usual fish and French fries for dinner. On the way home, we stopped at the fried fish store, and Grandma P and Lily ran inside to pick up our order.

While we waited in the car, Grandpa turned to me and asked, "Alex, tell me about Brandon the bully."

I jumped right in. "Well, Grandpa, he's bigger than me. It seems like he might have failed a grade or was held back. He wears blue jeans and a T-shirt every day. He has brown hair and dark eyes. And he always wears white sneakers."

I spoke quickly, excitedly, thinking maybe Grandpa was going to help me get back at him.

Grandpa nodded but kept asking more questions. "Where did you meet Brandon?"

"At the bus stop," I answered. "He lives one block over from me. He doesn't play sports, so he never joins our Nerf football or wiffle ball games. He's kind of a loner. His house isn't the nicest, and he told me his parents argue all the time. His dad drinks a lot."

Grandpa raised an eyebrow. "He *does*?"

I nodded.

"How do you know?"

I hesitated, then said, "He told me. One morning, we got to the bus stop early—before anyone else showed up. I was complaining about having to bring a bagged lunch instead of getting lunch money. And he just… said something weird."

Grandpa leaned in. "What did he say?"

"He said, 'I should be happy I have someone to make me lunch. And even *happier* that my father doesn't drink and hit me."

Grandpa sat quietly for a moment, then asked, "When did he start bullying you?"

"That same day," I said. "It was like… he was mad at me."

Grandpa frowned. "Mad at you… or maybe *sad* because he had no lunch?"

I shook my head. "No. He *told* me—he was going to take my lunch every day."

"Oh…" Grandpa murmured. "And what else did he do?"

I took a deep breath, getting more animated as I talked. "He gave me *nuggies*—he'd lock me in a headlock and rub his knuckles into my scalp. He threatened me at my locker. Emily tried to stand up for me, and he threatened her too—he *stole* her lunch money. I tried to protect her, but he twisted my arm, shoved me to the ground, and told me to *stay down*—right in front of everyone."

I clenched my fists. "I was so embarrassed. The other kids laughed and mocked me. I just wanted to *kill* him, Grandpa."

Grandpa sighed. "Yes… and you said that earlier, Alex You want to kill the bully, Brandon."

I nodded, still angry.

Just then, Grandma P and Lily returned, carrying our food.

Grandpa started the car. "Alright," he said, "let's go home and eat our fish dinner. After that, we'll continue our talk about Brandon."

Then he glanced at me and added, "And we'll get ready for the gun range tomorrow."

Chapter 6

I was excited about going to the gun range but confused by my grandpa's questions. Why did he care so much about Brandon? I was the one dealing with the problem of him bullying me. It felt like grandpa was asking those questions to get some answer, but they were all about Brandon.

After finishing my meal, I brought my plate from the table to the sink, and grandpa said, "Come on, Alex, let's go to the basement to continue our talk and get our guns and ammunition ready for tomorrow." We went downstairs to grandpa P's basement. It was a typical basement—there was a washer, a dryer, a fruit cellar for dry storage, a lot of Christmas and holiday decorations, and in the back, up against the wall, a big black box. That's what it looked like to me until grandpa started moving boxes out of the way, revealing the front of a safe. It was a large black safe, and I was shocked. I'd always wondered what was inside it, but my curiosity hadn't been strong enough to move the heavy boxes blocking it. I'd always thought it was just another storage box, but now I realized it wasn't.

Grandpa moved the last box, then said, "Alex, come here and look at this." He began explaining, "All guns and ammo should always be kept in a locked safe until you're ready to use them." I was confused at first, but then he reminded me, "Do you remember the lesson you learned with your sister, when you made fun of her and mocked her braces? Calling her tin grin and brace face?" He started, leading me on, "If you don't have anything nice to—"

I immediately interrupted and blurted out, "—then you don't say anything at all." I repeated it to show him I knew the answer: "If you don't have anything nice to say, then you shouldn't say anything at all."

I started feeling a little better, and grandpa continued. Of course, that didn't stop me from asking one of my favorite questions as a kid: "Why keep the guns in the safe grandpa?" He knew he had my attention and smiled as he spun the knob on the safe. "This is a safety measure for all people who have guns and ammo around," he explained. "You don't want them to be stolen or fall into the hands of people who aren't properly trained on how to handle them."

I asked, "Will I get my own safe to keep my gun and ammo too?"

He replied, "Well, we have to teach you how to handle the safe you have—your mouth. You can use my safe to store your gun when you get one."

Just then, I heard a click, and grandpa opened the safe, saying, "There we go." He placed his hand on a big handle beneath the lock dial and pushed it down. The door swung open, and he said under his breath in a light tone, "Here are my friends."

I didn't understand, so I asked, "Why are they your friends?"

He replied, "You have to respect your gun. You have to take care of it, store it properly, and keep it clean. When you take care of it properly, it shows you care about it and the proper storage and use of it."

I was shocked when he swung the safe door open to reveal all kinds of guns and ammo. There were long guns, short guns, big bullets, small bullets—I was in awe. My grandfather had always been cool to me, but this took his coolness to a whole new level. I felt excited and scared at the same time. I had never seen this side of grandpa, and he was about to surprise me even more. I felt like a kid at Christmas, with all these new toys in front of me.

I worked my way around to the side of him, reaching into the safe and asking, "Can we play with them? Do they have bullets in them?"

He gently grabbed my arm, held it, and looked right into my eyes. "No, Alex, guns and bullets are not toys. Why would you try to grab one if no one's ever taught you how to handle it? I know you're excited, but you have to use your brain first and foremost when you're around guns."

He slowly moved my arm back and let go. He pulled up a stool next to him and said, "Okay, sit down here next to me. Let's talk."

So I sat down, and he reached into the safe and pulled out the coolest-looking gun I'd ever seen. I had only seen guns on TV and in the video games I've played play before, but seeing it in person made me think, *This is awesome. I'm never going to be harassed and bullied at the bus stop, on the bus, at my locker, at lunch, in gym class, or in front of anyone again. I was going to kill the bully.*

Grandpa noticed the smile on my face and the twinkle in my eyes. He said, "Pretty neat, huh?" He then pulled out his handgun and explained, "The first thing you do when you pick up a gun is make sure it's not loaded." He held it up and showed me how to check if it was loaded. That was my first gun lesson, and it was very cool. I started to feel more powerful already.

He handed me the gun after verifying it wasn't loaded. I was in shock. The gun was so heavy that the weight of it pushed my arm down when he handed it to me. I had only ever had plastic guns when I played cops and robbers with my friends on the street.

He smiled and said, "It's heavy, huh?" I asked if they made smaller, lighter guns for kids. He said, "They make many different kinds of guns for people who know how to handle them and be responsible for their guns and ammo. If you don't learn these things and don't respect your gun, you shouldn't have one." Grandpa said this in a very serious tone. I knew he meant it.

I was way ahead of him, though. I was thinking things like, *How am I going to get this into school? Should I shoot the bully* Brandon, *or should I make all the teachers and kids pay for either ignoring what* Brandon *did or laughing along with him when he picked on me?* I didn't ask grandpa any of these questions, though, because he was already reaching for the bullets.

I asked as he pulled the bullets out, "What are those big long guns, grandpa? Will I learn how to use those too?"

"Eventually, Alex One thing at a time. Those longer guns are shotguns. Each gun and its ammunition have a specific design and purpose, and there's a lot for you to learn. Today, we're going to start with a handgun." He grabbed another handgun, bigger and heavier. When he handed it to me, I realized how heavy it was and said, "This is too heavy."

He laughed and said, "Yes, this one is mine." He grabbed the bullets for it, which came in a bigger box than mine.

He held his hands out and said, "Give me your gun, Alex." I handed it to him, and he started explaining each part of the gun— the grip, the front and rear sights, the barrel, the muzzle, the trigger, the cylinder, the safety lock, and the frame. "These are the stationary parts of the gun."

I couldn't believe how much he knew, and I couldn't believe he was teaching me these things. I was really starting to believe that I would be able to deal with anyone.

Grandpa continued explaining the gun. The first items we discussed were the stationary parts. He grabbed my gun again and said, "Okay, let's take a look at the moving parts." He continued explaining each item, telling me the name and its purpose: the trigger, the cylinder, the ejector, the extractor, the cylinder release, and finally, the hammer. I was in awe. I couldn't believe how much grandpa knew about guns. But he wasn't done.

"Alright, give me your gun, let's put it back in the safe, and talk about my gun," he said. My eyes lit up. His gun was different. It was big and cool-looking. He started with the grip again, explaining each component in detail. "This is the magazine, here is the magazine release, the slide, the safety de-locking lever, the frame, the takedown lever, the slide stop, the recoil spring, and guide."

I was in shock. I couldn't believe how much grandpa knew about guns. Then he blew my mind. He took the gun in his hand and started to take it apart while explaining. "I mentioned to you earlier that you also have to clean your gun. Each gun you own has to be cleaned properly when you're done using it." He continued taking the gun apart until it lay on the bench in pieces.

I asked, "Is it broken?"

He smiled with a soft giggle and said, "No, Alex, this is what you have to do to clean this particular handgun." He added, "It's always best to get in the habit of cleaning your gun after you use it, so it's always ready to go." He asked me if I was understanding everything and if I had any questions.

I asked, "I'm not going to have to use your gun, am I? I like the smaller one; it's a bit lighter than yours."

"No, you will use your gun with bullets, and I will use mine," he replied. He explained this as he put his gun back together in seconds.

He slapped parts back together on that gun so fast I could tell it wasn't the first time he'd done it. I was excited to learn this stuff, but I was more surprised by what a total badass my grandfather was. I now saw him in a way I never had before. He was super cool. Especially because he was helping me with my bully problem and teaching me the tools to resolve the issue.

He took my gun back and put it in the safe, and spun the combination dial. I asked him, "Am I going to get to know the combination of this lock?"

He explained simply, "Alex, I hope you never share your lock combination with anyone in your life. Locks are designed to make sure only the person with the key or combination can gain access to what's locked up. That's yours. Do you understand?"

"Yes, grandpa," I replied in a quiet, reserved tone.

We headed back upstairs, and I was already thinking about my gun, bullets, and the gun range we were going to in the morning. We watched television for the rest of the night, but I couldn't wait for the morning to come. I went to bed that night thinking of all the times Brandon the bully had messed with me— Emily, my friends, and all the teachers and other students who didn't help. I realized as I was laying there that I hadn't found out how many bullets went into my gun. I thought to myself, *Will I have enough bullets?* I fell asleep thinking about my gun lesson and bullets.

When morning came, it didn't take much to get me up. In fact, I think I was up before anyone else in the house. We all had our morning breakfast and discussed the upcoming activities for the day. The plan was for Grandma P and Lily to go to the farmers' market, and Grandpa P and I were going to the gun range. The girls were going to take Grandma's car to the market, and Grandpa and I were going to take his car to the range.

Grandpa said, "Alright, Alex, let me grab a duffel bag to put our guns and ammo in." We went to the basement, loaded everything up, and were on our way.

Grandpa started talking about strange things as we walked toward the car. He explained how proud he was of me for confronting my bully issue at school and said my effort to resolve it was commendable. This made me feel good at first. Then, the reality began to set in: my grandpa was taking me to the gun range to learn how to shoot a gun so I could shoot the people who participated in the bullying I faced at school. I started getting concerned and began asking questions.

"Grandpa, how many bullets does my gun hold?"

"Six," he replied.

I asked, "Well, what if I miss and run out of bullets and need more?"

He said, "Last night you learned about guns, the parts of a gun, and today you'll learn about ammunition and how to load your gun.

Don't worry, you'll never run out of bullets after you learn what we do today."

I thought to myself, *This is so cool. I'm gonna be the fixer, just like on TV and in the movies we watched. When there's an issue, they call the guy who goes by the nickname 'The Fixer' for the answer. He does whatever it takes to resolve the issue.*

I said it out loud to Grandpa, "I'm gonna be the fixer, Grandpa, just like the one we watched on TV."

He laughed out loud as he patted me on the head and said, "Oh yes, Alex, you'll be the fixer."

I was excited and scared at the same time. Keep in mind, I hadn't loaded or fired a gun yet. I loved Grandpa for putting such faith in me, but I was scared. I had so many questions. I chose not to ask them until we got to the gun range. I simply said, "I'm the fixer; if there's an issue, I'll now have the answer."

Grandpa laughed again, patted me on the head, and said, "Yes, Alex, you'll be the fixer." He continued with some statements and questions he had for me.

"Ya know, Alex, last night you had your first introduction to guns and ammo. You're a quick learner, but you need to learn much more before you can get your own gun. Do you have any questions about gun storage, guns, and bullets I've taught you about so far?"

I replied, "No, Grandpa. I get it."

He continued, "It's important you learn the rules and safety standards of gun ownership first. Then it's more important that you learn the proper way to use them and when to use them. If you have any questions today, it's important that you ask them, and I want you to feel comfortable asking me anything. You get it?"

"Yes, Grandpa," I replied.

He continued with more questions. "Do you remember when I showed you the parts of a gun yesterday?"

I replied in a low, questioning tone, "Yes."

He asked, "Do you know what the grip is for?"

I responded more confidently this time, "Yes."

He asked, "Do you remember how important the trigger safety lock is from the moment you grab the gun by the grip?"

I replied, "Yes, we always make sure our safety lock is on when handling a gun."

He smiled and said, "Good, good. You're doing well. What does the barrel do?"

I said, "That's the long, round, hollow piece that sits on the frame of the gun, where the bullet flies out of."

His response made me feel good.

He said, "Wow, you remembered the frame. I was going to ask you what the barrel sat on. Very good." Then he followed up with, "What did you forget?" He caught me off guard—I didn't know the answer. I hesitated and then responded with a question, "The bullets?"

He asked, "And where do the bullets go?" I replied excitedly, "Oh, I remember! The round thing... the chamber?" I asked, unsure.

He smiled and said, "Close. The chamber is part of the cylinder. The cylinder holds the chamber, and the chamber holds the bullets. Don't worry—it will make more sense when we load the gun at the range, and you actually touch and see the parts. Great job so far. We'll spend more time on the different parts to help you remember them and learn how to use them when we get to the range."

Grandpa continued, and his tone started to resemble a familiar lecture I'd heard before about my gaming habits. "Now, I know you spend a lot of time playing those shoot-'em-up killing games on your Xbox or PlayStation. Do you have fun with that?"

His question threw me off a bit. "Yeah, that's why mom yells at me to go outside and play," I responded.

He kept asking questions. "What do you like about it?"

I didn't have to think about my answer. I was visibly excited as I explained. "It's awesome, Grandpa! You would love it! You can play alone or with a team, depending on which game you're playing. You get to shoot people for points or money to buy ammo and guns. There are different levels to the game, and you move through them to try to win. I love the power it gives me. I make myself believe the people I'm shooting are like Brandon the bully, my teachers, or anyone else who bothers me."

Grandpa pulled the car to the side of the road and turned on the flashers. I was scared—I thought I was in trouble for what I said. But what he said next threw me off course.

"Well, games are for fun, and guns can be even more fun when used properly and for the right reasons. Do you know that you're already a gun owner, Alex?"

I thought I knew the answer, so I responded quickly, "Yeah, I have my toy guns and the guns in my games, but they don't work in real life."

He smiled. "Yes, those are definitely guns that you own and play with, but that's not the gun I'm talking about. Think, Alex. What gun haven't you used yet?"

I was completely lost and starting to get nervous. We were parked on the side of the road, and Grandpa was asking me a question I had no clue how to answer. I gave up and said, "No, Grandpa, I don't own any other gun. What do you mean?"

He immediately turned off the flashers and said, "Hold on, let's get someplace safe." He drove us into the nearby shopping plaza, parked the car, and turned sideways in his seat to look directly into my eyes with a serious expression.

"Alex, Alex, Alex," he said. "You are the gun."

I was stunned. "I am the gun, Grandpa?"

"In fact, you're more powerful than any real gun or the ones you play with in your games."

"I don't understand, Grandpa. People can't be guns."

"Oh yes, they can, Alex. Remember how we learned about the components of a gun last night? The grip, the trigger, the trigger guard, the trigger safety, the barrel, the cylinder/chamber, and the bullets?"

"Yes, Grandpa, we went through that."

"Great. Well, the super powerful gun that you already own is inside you, and it's made up of components, just like the guns we'll fire at the range. Want to take a guess as to what they are?"

I just shrugged my shoulders and held my hands up. "I don't know what you're saying. It doesn't make sense."

"Okay, let me explain why you are the gun and how your body makes up the components of the gun you already own. The frame of the gun is your body. The grip of the gun is your brain. The front and rear sights on the gun are your eyes and ears. Your thoughts are the cylinder, and your words are the bullets. It's very important that you understand how to use the gun you already own. You are the gun."

I was confused and losing interest. I wasn't sure where this conversation was headed, so I just replied, "Okay, Grandpa, I am the gun. Are we still going to the gun range?"

He smiled. "Soon enough. But tell me, what purpose do the components of the gun you already have serve? What do they do?"

"You want to make sure their functions are just like the handgun's parts you've learned about," he said.

I slouched in my seat, looked sideways at him, and muttered, "We're not going to the range, are we?"

"No, no, no. Don't worry, we'll go, but let's finish talking about this first."

"But Grandpa, I don't know what you're talking about. Can't you just tell me?"

"Absolutely. And I think you'll know how to fire your first gun—the one you already own—long before we get to the range. Okay, the gun has a frame that holds it all together, just like your body, right?"

"Yes, I guess."

"Well, if there was no frame to the gun and no body, where would all the other components fit?"

I thought for a second. "Oh, I get it. We need the frame for the real gun, and my body is the frame of my internal gun?"

He smiled. "Now you're getting it." I went from slouching in my seat to sitting up straight, paying attention again. I was getting excited.

"The front and rear sights are used for aiming a gun, and they're on the gun you'll use today. What are your internal gun sights?"

I knew the answer right away. "My eyes!"

"That's half right," he said. "What else?"

I answered quickly, excited, "Both eyes! I won't close one eye to aim. I'll keep both eyes open."

He smiled and said, "Slow down, slow down. It's your ears. Just think about it—if the frame is your body and the front and rear sights are your eyes and ears, then that would make the trigger your mouth, and the bullets are your words. The safety lock is your brain, and the grip represents your thoughts. You never grab the grip of a gun unless you have clear thoughts."

"The components of your internal gun are just like a real gun. Your internal gun is much more powerful than any handgun or any gun you'll ever see or use. You want to be sure to exercise the same precaution as you would when firing a regular gun."

He asked if I was following along and if I had any questions. I nodded, and he quickly said, "Good. Now let's fire your gun right here in the car."

I was confused. "What? In the car? How? What do you mean?"

"Your bad thoughts about your bully, the teachers, and the other students represent the grip. All the stuff they do to you every day makes you want to grab the grip of a gun, right?"

"Yes, Grandpa, they brought this on."

"Great! You've already put your internal gun's sights and frame to use."

"The frame equals your body, and the sights equal your eyes and ears. You've told me you don't like what's going on at school, and you know this because you saw it, heard it, and felt it. Don't you?"

I answered with a long, drawn-out, "Yes…" in a quiet, reserved tone. I knew he was going somewhere with our talk, but I wasn't sure exactly where.

He continued, "This leaves the trigger and the bullets. The trigger of your internal gun is your mouth, and your words are your bullets. You see, you've already been shot by everyone else's internal gun. It's hard to blame them when they just don't know how to use it. So, what do you do?"

Then, he completely switched gears on me. "What do you know about Brandon, the bully, Alex?"

I quickly responded, "He's mean, he pokes me, hits me, and makes fun of me in front of other students and teachers until they all laugh at me." I continued, "He wears the same jeans, T-shirt, and sneakers every day. His hair is messy, and he never has lunch. He steals my lunch or my lunch money—or someone else's lunch— every day."

Grandpa started shifting in his seat, looking uncomfortable. He asked, "Do you think using a real gun or your internal gun will stop him?"

I didn't hesitate with my response. "A gun! Words don't stop bullies; they just get meaner and do more mean things."

Grandpa nodded and said, "I know this situation is very hard for you, Alex. This is probably the first bully you've ever had to deal with, and it definitely won't be the last bully you'll meet or have to deal with. Do you know what makes a person a bully?"

I thought for a moment and said, "Yeah, they're mean and have no feelings."

Grandpa responded, "That's the end result, but the truth is, you should feel bad for the bully. Think about it: people who feel the need to bully others are typically acting out due to things happening in their lives—things they have no control over or can't figure out how to stop. Did you ever think the bully might just want a friend or someone to talk to?"

I thought for a moment and grandpa asked, "Who does Brandon eat lunch with every day?"

"No one. He eats alone. I don't think he has any friends. He's kind of a loner. I was nice to him at the bus stop the first few days of school, but when I asked why he always has that weird look on his face, like he's always mad, he immediately changed and got mad at me."

"Well, I already told you the first rule about your internal gun, Alex. If you don't have anything nice to say, then you shouldn't say anything at all."

"Okay, well with what you've explained to me, I can see why you want to shoot him. The question is, which gun would you use?"

I was confused again and asked, "Which gun?"

"Well, Alex, it's only legal to use a handgun for shooting targets and hunting once you have a license. On the other hand, you can use your internal gun. Remember the components of your internal gun?"

I replied softly, "Yeah…"

"Well, you have to use your internal gun with the same safety and caution that you would use a real gun. Think about it: Brandon has been firing bullets at you from his internal gun since the first day of school. Are you ready to learn how to fire back?"

"I believe you want to learn how to use your internal gun—but in a very different way than Brandon, your bully. As you go through life, you'll run into bullies at school, at work, and maybe even within your circle of friends. You want to use your internal gun for good, never for bad. Your words are your bullets. If you're thinking of shooting your mouth off and doing what the bully did to you, you'll only make things worse."

"You have to use different bullets—or words, right?" I asked, still confused.

"Exactly," Grandpa said. "You need to be kind. I want you to be Brandon's friend. I want you to say, 'Good morning, Brandon,' and ask how he's doing at the bus stop. Talk to him on the bus ride to school. Make a sandwich and bring it to school for him. He'll stop stealing yours and will probably appreciate it. Sit with him at lunch, listen to him, and be a friend to him. This may be hard at first, and it may not work right away. Another way to deal with a bully is to avoid them altogether. But the more you avoid a problem in life, the worse it gets. Do you understand why people become bullies?"

"Yes, Grandpa, I think. But what do I do?"

"Words don't kill people."

"No, Alex, they don't. But they're much more powerful than any bullets you'll ever put into a gun. Just like there are different bullets for a gun, there are different 'bullets' or words for your internal gun. You can 'kill' the bully with kindness. Kind words, kind gestures, supportive listening, and being nice all the time. Think about it. Now that you know why a bully acts the way they do, think about how bullying affected you and made you feel. The funny thing is, your bully might even become your best friend."

"But what if they don't, Grandpa? What if they keep being mean?"

"It might not work right away. It may take a few days. But you can continue to be nice and say, 'Hey, I just want to be friends. I understand if you don't want to be. I'll leave you alone, but I'm here for you if you ever need a friend.' Then walk away and keep the door open to friendship. You should always act friendly and polite, even if they're still a bully. The truth is, you should feel bad for them. Bullies are usually very insecure people. They put others down to make themselves feel better. They could be dealing with some type of pain."

"The bully is acting out because they have no solution to the problem they're dealing with. Ninety percent of the time, it's a cry for help. They just want a friend or someone to listen to them. You should know that this won't work with everyone. The other 10% of the time, you just have to walk away. But this doesn't change how you 'kill the bully.' You can fix anything now that you know how to carry and shoot your internal gun."

"Does that excite you or not?"

"Yes! I'm not the fixer now. I'm not going to shoot anyone to fix them."

Then Grandpa asked, "What if you use your internal gun and all the parts that make up your gun? You'll shoot them with your word bullets, and your words and actions will have more impact than any normal gun or bullets."

"You know Tom, Grandpa's friend, right?"

"Yes, the guy you golf with all the time."

Grandpa explained, "He was my bully. I killed my bully with kindness, and we've now been friends for 30 years. I learned about my internal gun the same way you have over the past couple of days."

"Now you still think you need a gun to be 'The Fixer'?"

"Yes, I still need a gun—but not one of those in the bag. I have my internal gun, more powerful than any gun or bullet in the world."

"That's great, Alex. I'm so proud of you," Grandpa said, patting me on the shoulder. "Well, I guess your dreams of becoming the Fixer will have to stay in your games."

"No, I don't think so, Grandpa. I am and always will be 'The Fixer.'"

I could see Grandpa was getting a little choked up as he started the car. "Okay? We're getting ready to go to the gun range and teach you how to shoot a real gun."

"Hey, Grandpa, can we go hit golf balls instead? I don't need a gun, bullets, or gun training. I have the most powerful gun in the world: my internal gun. And now, I have all the bullets I need."

"You are awesome, Grandpa."

"So are you, Alex. You're a very smart kid. Let's go golfing."

Chapter 7

This is just one of many bullying stories that exist in our world today. Bullies come in all forms—male, female, teacher, boss, and more. It's unfortunate, but some people have had bad experiences in life that cause them to lash out at others, sometimes even those they love. Bullies feel bad about themselves, and they put others down, make fun of them, or mock them to build themselves up. You will now be able to immediately recognize someone in pain that is crying out for help. The bully. You now know how to kill the bully too.

Kill them with kindness, you never know you just might meet your next best friend.

9 781969 644672